The Strange Lapses of Larry Loman by Edgar Wallace

Richard Horatio Edgar Wallace was born on the 1st April 1875 in Greenwich, London. Leaving school at 12 because of truancy, by the age of fifteen he had experience; selling newspapers, as a worker in a rubber factory, as a shoe shop assistant, as a milk delivery boy and as a ship's cook.

By 1894 he was engaged but broke it off to join the Infantry being posted to South Africa. He also changed his name to Edgar Wallace which he took from Lew Wallace, the author of Ben-Hur.

In Cape Town in 1898 he met Rudyard Kipling and was inspired to begin writing. His first collection of ballads, The Mission that Failed! was enough of a success that in 1899 he paid his way out of the armed forces in order to turn to writing full time.

By 1904 he had completed his first thriller, The Four Just Men. Since nobody would publish it he resorted to setting up his own publishing company which he called Tallis Press.

In 1911 his Congolese stories were published in a collection called Sanders of the River, which became a bestseller. He also started his own racing papers, Bibury's and R. E. Walton's Weekly, eventually buying his own racehorses and losing thousands gambling. A life of exceptionally high income was also mirrored with exceptionally large spending and debts.

Wallace now began to take his career as a fiction writer more seriously, signing with Hodder and Stoughton in 1921. He was marketed as the 'King of Thrillers' and they gave him the trademark image of a trilby, a cigarette holder and a yellow Rolls Royce. He was truly prolific, capable not only of producing a 70,000 word novel in three days but of doing three novels in a row in such a manner. It was estimated that by 1928 one in four books being read was written by Wallace, for alongside his famous thrillers he wrote variously in other genres, including science fiction, non-fiction accounts of WWI which amounted to ten volumes and screen plays. Eventually he would reach the remarkable total of 170 novels, 18 stage plays and 957 short stories.

Wallace became chairman of the Press Club which to this day holds an annual Edgar Wallace Award, rewarding 'excellence in writing'.

Diagnosed with diabetes his health deteriorated and he soon entered a coma and died of his condition and double pneumonia on the 7th of February 1932 in North Maple Drive, Beverly Hills. He was buried near his home in England at Chalklands, Bourne End, in Buckinghamshire.

Index of Contents

CHAPTER I

THE CRIME TRUST

Sir George Grayborn leaned back in his chair and looked from the young man who sat at the other side of his desk to the notes on pulse, respiration, reflexes, et cetera, he had scribbled on his pad.

"Well?" Larry Loman's tone was a little truculent.

"My dear sir," said Sir George slowly, "yours is a very peculiar case, and I hardly know what to advise you."

"Do you think I am going mad?" asked the young man with a certain cheerfulness.

He took a gold cigarette case from his pocket and carefully extracted and lit a cigarette.

"I suppose I shan't horrify your subsequent patients?"

Sir George smiled.

"No, you won't horrify them, and you can't horrify me. I recognize in you a unique specimen of the human race apart from being a very interesting case, and I am grateful to the circumstances which brought you here at all."

"It was rather a fluke," laughed Larry, "Everybody knows—that is to say, everybody who is interested in me—that my memory has been going all wrong, and, knowing this, some unknown friend had sent me a copy of your work on 'Mnemotechny.'"

The physician inclined his head.

"I had heard of you, of course," he said politely. "In our profession one is obliged to keep in-touch with current happenings."

"Honestly, Sir George," interrupted the young man, growing serious of a sudden, "is there anything radically wrong with me?"

The physician nodded.

"Yes and no," he said. "I gather that somewhere in your wanderings you have struck a very bad malaria patch."

"That is right," nodded the other; "up in the Aruwimi country, four years ago. I contracted there all kinds of' fever. Is there any symptom of malaria?"

"No," said the other carefully, "not especially, but your mental condition is one which frequently follows either a bad fever or a bad bout of nerves."

"You can cut out all the nerve theories," said the young man with decision, "and put it down to fever. The only thing I am worried about is this." He leaned over the table and emphasized each point by tapping a little tattoo upon the immaculate blotting pad of the consultant. "I am up to my eyes in work—serious and dangerous work. I want all my wits about me because I have a tricky crowd to deal with. Now, if I am not responsible for my actions—"

"Believe me," said Sir George, "you will always be responsible for your actions. The only thing is—you will not remember everything you do. You are suffering from periodic amnesia, which does not seem to be merely an instance of amnesic aphasia. You will find from time to time whole periods, probably for four or five hours, of your day wiped out of your recollection."

"You mean to say that I shall wake up one fine morning and forget what happened the previous evening?"

Sir George nodded.

"And more than that. You may go out one day and retain a perfect recollection of what you do until, say, twelve o'clock. You will be able to recall vividly everything that happened from four o'clock onward, but the period between twelve and four, or whatever time the attack occupies, will be an absolute blank. It may last for four, five, or six hours. It may even last a day. You will be perfectly rational—just as rational as you are now—but whatever the period is will be blotted entirely from your recollection."

He rose, walked to his bookcase, and took down a small skull, and, placing it upon the writing table, picked up a pencil and traced an irregular patch upon the whitened bones.

"Behind here," he said, "is what is known as 'Brochia's Convolution,' that department of the brain which has to deal with memory. A portion of that convolution in your head is diseased."

"That sounds rather alarming," said the young man, with a frown.

"It is not quite so alarming as it sounds, because it need not be a chronic disease, and it is quite possible, by a course of treatment, to restore yourself to a normal state. See me after every bad lapse. You ought, of course, to take a holiday."

"That is impossible," said the young man, shaking his head; "wholly impossible! If you assure me that I shan't make a fool of myself during the period of lapse—"

"I can only assure you that you will be normal," said the professor, "and if you are liable to make a fool of yourself in normal moments you will certainly be just as foolish. It will only be in your recollection of happenings that you will fail—especially of those happenings which begin with some event of an exciting character. You probably experience a curious, buzzing noise in your ears, and that is about your last recollection before your mind goes blank? I thought so. I suggest that you should carry with you a small notebook, and acquire the habit of jotting down from hour to hour a little diary of impressions, engagements, et cetera."

Larry shook his head as he rose to go.

"That also is impossible," he said. "I dare not keep written records—especially of this case."

"I will not be so indiscreet as to inquire what the 'case' is," said Sir George with a little smile as he led the way to the door.

"That's the dickens of it!" said Larry ruefully. "Not that it is a secret," he added quickly. "Even Harley Street has heard of 'The Trust.'"

The physician raised his eyebrows.

"Surely you aren't a believer in the existence of a romantic robber band?" he said. "I thought it was a newspaper fabrication. They seem to credit every crime, where the perpetrator is not brought to justice, to that organization."

"I not only 'believe,'" said the other emphatically, "but I know, and unfortunately I am the only man who has all the strings of the counter-work in my hand. I told you I could not keep records, and I will explain why. How many times do you think my bureau has been burgled? Six times in four months! Every document I have has been read and reread. Even the record office of the department has not escaped attention. I tell you, The Trust is a very real organization which has bought up the services of every professional criminal in England. Look at the crime tables in the commissioner's annual report. A fifty-percent decrease of serious burglaries in point of numbers, an eight- percent decrease of ladder larcenies, a ninety-per-cent decrease in big-gang forgeries. Why? Because the report only shows convictions, and those men are no longer caught. They are in the service of The Trust. They get more money than they ever made before. The job is made safer, and if they are caught they don't have to make a collection among their friends to secure a third-rate lawyer; they have the best legal advice that money can buy. Goddard, the burglar, was defended by an ex-attorney general at the Winchester Assizes the other day, and the fees must have run into a thousand pounds! If they are sent to prison, their wives are in receipt of a handsome separation allowance. Do you wonder that The Trust is recruiting the best men in the business? We are fighting the combine, and we ought to beat it—if my infernal memory had not started playing tricks!"

He threw out his hands in a gesture of despair.

"It is tragic; I am on the very edge of discovery! In a month I should drive a wedge into the gang as would split it from top to bottom—and I'll do it yet!"

"Yours is the kind of case that the unspeakable Stinie is always touting for," said Sir George, and, seeing that his words conveyed no meaning to the visitor, he went on: "Stinie is a doctor of sorts; I have had no opportunity of testing his ability. He holds a foreign degree which is not accepted here, but I must say, qualified or not, he is running one of the best nursing homes in London and he professes to make a specialty of cases like yours."

There was a discreet knock at the door, and Sir George's butler entered with a card on a tray. The specialist took up the card and adjusted his pince-nez. His eyebrows went up, and he uttered an exclamation of surprise.

"Talk of the devil—" he said. "Here is the very man! Would you like to see him?"

"Not professionally," said Larry hastily.

"I wonder what he wants? This is the first time he has come to me. Ask the gentleman in."

The butler departed, and returned in a few seconds, ushering in a stout man immaculately dressed. He had large dark eyes and stiff, upstanding hair and a mustache that gave evidence of consistent and careful training.

"Ah, Sir George, you will pardon me," he said, speaking with the slightest foreign accent, "I desire you to see one of my patients."

He bowed to Larry, who returned the salutation.

"It is not possible," said the newcomer with an exaggerated shrug, "that I should ask you for a consultation, since I am not recognize' in this country, but if you would be so kind and good to see a most unfortunate fellow with nerve, I should be happy."

All the time he was speaking to the physician his eyes were fixed upon Larry with a blank stare. Sir George hesitated and made what to Larry was an extremely lame excuse. Then followed an animated discussion on the one part, somewhat cold and unresponsive on the other. The little man now devoted the whole of his attention to the doctor, and pleaded, cajoled, smiled, was desolate, and did not remain still a single second.

"A persistent beggar," said Sir George after he had gone. "What do you think of him?"

"I have met the type before," said Larry carelessly. "Now I am afraid I must go."

He passed into the sunshine of Harley Street, a little disconcerted, but by no means alarmed. His car was waiting unattended, and he cranked it up, and Sir George, watching from the study window, saw him disappear in an evil-looking cloud of smoke.

Larry had a flat near Berkeley Square, and thither he drove, his mind occupied with the interview.

He brought his car to a standstill and jumped out.

"Has anybody called?" he asked the liveried porter.

"Yes, sir; a gentleman came about five minutes ago."

Larry nodded, and stepped into the elevator.

The man who sprawled in a big club chair in Larry's sitting room, sucking reflectively at the end of a rank cigar, was stout and unshaven. His dress was untidy, his thin hair unkempt, a faint discoloration under one eye suggested a recent injury, and the scarred and shiny knuckles of the hand—by no means cleanly—which removed the cigar stump, confirmed its owner's pugnacity.

"Ah, Croop," said Larry, walking across the room and throwing open the windows, "you're on time. Throw that cigar away and help yourself to something that smells less like a burning soap factory."

The man sat up with a grin, and, pitching the stump into the fireplace, fumbled in the box which his host offered.

"Now," said Larry, "what have you got to tell me? By the way, when did you come out of prison?"

"The last time? Months ago," said Mr. Croop proudly. "I'm straight now, Mr. Loman; got a job lookin' after a boxin' booth. There ain't much money in it, but, as I ses, 'honesty,' I ses, 'is the best policy.' I could make pots of stuff, Mr. Loman; I'm the kind of feller The Trust wants. Look at that!" He held out his grimy paw triumphantly.

"That's the 'and that drew the finest five-pun notes that was ever put on the market; ten years I got for it."

Larry nodded. He was perched on the window seat, and was eying his visitor with interest.

"You're the finest forger in the world," he admitted.

The gratified Mr. Croop purred. "Praise from Sir 'Erbert—"

"Hubert," corrected Larry. "That's all right, Croop. Now I want you to look at this."

He took a note from his wallet and passed it across to the man, who rose with a grunt from his seat and crossed to the window.

"Phony," he said. "Bank of Chilagua; very difficult to draw, owin' to the cross hatchin' under the number, but it's phony all right."

"Why are you so sure it's a forgery?"

Mr. Croop smiled.

"Wrong shade of green," he said. "I've got a wonderful eye for color, Mr. Loman."

"You're quite right," said the detective, replacing the note in his case. "Fortunately there are not as yet many in circulation. You said just now," he went on, "that you could join The Trust, and you suggested that they would welcome you."

"That's right, sir," said Mr. Croop. "I'd get all the money I wanted."

"Why don't you join?" asked Larry.

Mr. Croop smiled. "'Honesty,' as I've said before—"

"Cut all that out," said Larry briefly, "and listen to the story of your misspent life. You don't join because you daren't. You told me just now you had ten years for forgery. How long did you serve?"

The man hesitated.

"You served one," said Larry; "the other nine years were remitted for services rendered. In other words, you turned State's evidence and convicted a brother forger, a man named Goul, and the reason you don't join The Trust is because Goul is out and already a member of it."

As he was speaking the man's face had grown a dirty white, and he dropped his eyes sullenly to the floor.

"That is why, when you offered to give me some information about the forgeries, I sent for you," Larry went on. "What do you know?"

"I know it is Goul's work," said. Mr. Croop doggedly, "and I know Goul has been seen about town lookin' like a bookmaker who had found a mug. Now, Mr. Loman," he said with vigor, "I can bring you to the man who supplied the plates for Goul. What is it worth? It isn't only the plates; it's the place they were delivered," he added. "You might get the whole crowd."

"Don't you know where they went?"

The man shook his head.

"When can I meet your friend?"

"You can meet him to-day, sir."

Larry thought for a moment, then took up his hat.

"Come on!" he said.

He opened the drawer of his desk and took out a revolver, which he slipped into his hip pocket.

"And you'll want it, I think," said Mr. Croop profoundly.

They went down in the elevator together, and strolled out onto the sunny pavement before the block, while the hall porter telephoned to the garage for Larry's car.

"I can tell you a lot, sir," said Croop earnestly, "but you will have to get me out of the country. The Trust is working these forgeries, but that is only a little thing. Why, sir, do you know—"

Larry heard a noise like "klock!" and something hit the wall behind him.

"A pistol with a Maxim silencer," said Larry's brain automatically.

He looked round quickly, and in that second took in a view of the street. There was a nurse walking on the other side of the road. There were two furniture men standing before an open door, resting over a large settee, which they were evidently moving in. There was a closed motor car a little way along the street, a butcher's boy....

"Klock!"

The muffled report was followed by a thud.

"That's done me," said the voice of Croop faintly.

He lurched against Larry and slipped in a huddled heap on the ground, and Larry, looking down, knew that the man was dead. He knelt down by the side of the murdered man, tearing open his waistcoat, and his hand was on the man's heart when he felt a curious buzzing and knew that the period of lapse had begun.

"Anyway, I know what is happening," said Larry, "and I shall remember this."

He was sitting before his dressing table, his head in his hands. He was dimly conscious that something had happened and that he had been through a remarkable experience. He knew that it was night, because he could see the shadow which the electric light cast upon the table. And something had happened—something remarkable.

The period of lapse had passed, and he was remembering things—Croop's white face, the pistol shot. He raised his head slowly, and caught the reflection of his face in the mirror before him, then leaped up with a cry. He was dressed in a Pierrot costume, a big white ruff was about his neck, a close-fitting black skullcap was on his head, and his face was whitened save for two straight black lines that represented his eyebrows and the carmine red of his lips. He saw something else. His left hand was enclosed in a thin handcuff, and a gaping steel link told him that in some way he had broken loose from detention.

He ran to the bell and pressed it, and almost immediately the door opened and his servant came in with a large tray bearing some cold meat, a bottle of wine, bread, cheese, and salad. The man put down the tray with an imperturbable face.

"How long have I been in, Wilkes?" asked Larry steadily.

"Half an hour," said the man.

"Did I come like—this?"

"Yes, sir," said the man gravely.

"Did I come alone?"

"Yes, sir," said the man. "I paid the cabman."

"Did I tell you where I had been?" asked Larry carelessly.

"To a fancy-dress ball, sir," said the man.

"Is that so?" said Larry. "Thank you, Wilkes; that will do."

When the man had gone he locked the door and slipped off the costume. He was fully dressed underneath, save for his coat. From the bureau he took a bunch of keys and released himself from the handcuff. With the aid of a towel and some cold cream, he removed the grease paint from his face, washed, and returned to his bedroom. He gathered that he had come straight to his bedroom with that object. He felt in his pockets for some clew. In his waistcoat pocket he found a small cartridge shell, recently fired, evidently from a Browning pistol. He recalled everything up to the death of Croop. After that his mind was a blank.

The cartridge shell he had evidently picked up somewhere, and he guessed that it was from this shell that the fatal bullet had been fired. That was something to begin with. The rest of his pockets revealed nothing. He had no money. His wallet was gone, as also was his coat, and he smiled as he remembered Sir George's suggestion that he should keep notes. His jaw ached a little, as though he had had a blow.

"'Curiouser and curiouser,'" quoted Larry.

He examined the Pierrot dress, and found a little tab behind the neck with the name of a well-known theatrical costumier, and a number, and went to the telephone. He knew it was useless calling up the costume shop, which would be closed at this hour, but fortunately the costumier was found at his private address.

"A Pierrot's costume?" he replied. "Yes, I have sent out several in the past few days, and I lent half a dozen this morning to an amateur Pierrot troupe that was entertaining some sick people. There ought to be a number attached to it."

"One-five-six," said Larry.

"That's it," came the prompt answer. "It was issued this morning, and it stands for fifteenth of the sixth. We always date our costumes because we charge for hire according to the time they are kept. They were lent to a man named Weatherby, of 63 Elgin Square, Bayswater."

Larry waited long enough to eat a hasty supper and change before he was in the street again.

The name of Mr. Weatherby, of Elgin Square, did not appear in the telephone book, but in a quarter of an hour a taxicab deposited the young man before a very gloomy house which had been divided up into maisonettes. Mr. Weatherby had not come home, explained the servant who answered his ring. Would he see Mrs. Weatherby?

Larry went upstairs to the ornate little drawing-room and introduced himself to a stout, pleasant lady. She confessed that she was the veritable wife of Mr. Weatherby, and regretted that that gentleman was not at home to receive him, and requested information on the reason for the visit.

"I am expecting him at any minute now," she said. "You know, he is a member of an amateur Pierrot troupe, and he and some of his friends are giving an entertainment at a nursing home."

"Do you know where?"

"I haven't the slightest idea," said the lady frankly, "though he did tell me."

There was a tinkle of the bell.

"That's him!" said Mrs. Weatherby, and went down to meet her lord, returning with an unhappy-looking man who greeted Larry with a sad smile.

"You are the police, I suppose?" he said.

"I am something like that," said Larry cautiously.

Mr. Weatherby turned to his wife.

"You don't know what trouble I've had this evening," he said. "Have they got him?" he asked the young man.

"I don't know yet," replied Larry more cautiously than ever.

"What has happened?" asked Mrs. Weatherby in alarm.

Her husband chuckled, seated himself, pulled out his pipe, charged and lighted it before he replied.

"It is the rummest go I've ever known. I will tell you the whole story, and I suppose you will want the complete yarn from beginning to end?"

Larry nodded.

"Me and a few friends," began Mr. Weatherby, "occasionally give little entertainments to the hospitals and nursing homes, and we had arranged to give one this evening. When we got to the place—Doctor Stinie's nursing home—you have probably heard of it?"

"Yes, yes," said Larry eagerly.

"Well, when we got there they gave us a room to dress and change in, and all the patients who were up were brought into the big dining hall downstairs. They gave us a dinner to start with. While we were at dinner there was a great rumpus. It appears that a dangerous lunatic that they had in one of the rooms next to the one we were dressing in had made his escape. He was so dangerous," said Mr. Weatherby impressively, "that there were guards in the corridors downstairs to prevent his getting away. This fellow, being, like all lunatics, a bit cunning, had broken away from his strait-jacket or whatever fastened him down, had sneaked into our room, dressed himself up as a Pierrot, and passed the guard. They thought it was one of our chaps, and didn't attempt to stop him."

"Do you know how the lunatic got into the building?" asked Larry.

Mr. Weatherby smiled.

"It is curious you should ask that," he said. "I am a bit of a detective myself, to tell you the truth, and I inquired of one of the patients. The lunatic escaped from another home, according to Doctor Stinie, and was only lured to Stinie's place this afternoon by a pretty nurse whom he saw in the street and followed. They'd never have got him then only she led the way up to a ward. He followed her up, and, seeing nothing but, as he thought, sick men lying in the beds, he ventured into the room. The moment he did so the men in the beds, who were attendants, jumped up and got him. One of the patients saw the struggle through the door, and, according to him, the lunatic half killed one man."

In a flash Larry had remembered the innocent-looking nurse who had been on the other side of the road when Croop was killed. He must have crossed in search of some clew and have found the cartridge shell near where she had been standing and followed her.

"Thank you," he said.

He went to the nearest telephone office and rang for a treasury number. At a quarter to eleven that night Stinie's nursing home was surrounded, and Larry, armed with the authority of the law, entered the building to find, however, that both Doctor Stinie and his pretty nurse had disappeared half an hour before the arrival of the police.

In a locked room, soberly inscribed, "Electrical Generating Room. Strictly Private," Larry discovered two very beautiful printing presses and a number of half-finished notes. More important, he found a man lying on one of the beds suffering from a broken ankle and a badly contused face.

Him Larry recognized.

"Mr. Goul, I presume?" he said pleasantly. "I shall want you for felony. How did you get your injuries?"

"A nice question to come from you!" said Mr. Goul with indignation.

Larry shook his head.

"I wish I could remember all that happened," he said regretfully.

The next story in the Wallace series will appear in the April 20th number of this magazine. It is called "The Affair of the Stokehole."

CHAPTER II

THE AFFAIR OF THE STOKEHOLE

Larry Loman, of the Criminal Intelligence Department, was called to a conference at headquarters, and went with a certain sense of disappointment and irritation, though there was no reason for a display of either of those emotions, for both his chief and the secretary of state, responsible for his department, had nothing but encouragement for him.

"You are not going to smash the Crime Trust in a day," said the chief commissioner for special services.

"I suppose there is no doubt about there being a Crime Trust?" asked the minister dubiously. "It seems such an extremely melodramatic idea, the sort of thing one reads in sensational stories."

"It is a very good idea from the criminal's point of view," said the commissioner quietly; "he has no worry. He is well supported, whether he is in prison or out. He is always excellently defended, and if he is convicted his unknown employers will take his case to the court of criminal appeal—if there is the slightest chance of a sentence being reduced or a trial being quashed. The man who brought together all these expert criminals—and the trust has no use for any other—was a genius. Could anything be neater than to run a forging plant in a nursing home, where all the rooms except two or three were occupied by genuine patients, and all the staff except the principal and a few of his friends were genuine nurses and doctors? How are things shaping, Larry?"

Larry Loman, his elbows on the table, his face between his hands, shook his head.

"We have settled the forgeries," he said a little hopelessly, "but the other departments of the trust are in full swing, and very successfully so."

"For example—" said the chief commissioner.

"The kidnapping and holding to ransom of Lord Frethermore's heir."

"I wanted to see you about that," said the minister; "do you think it is the work of the trust?"

"I am certain of it," said Larry emphatically. "Look at the price they are asking—sixty thousand pounds! Nobody but the trust would dare do it. Nobody but the trust has the organization which would enable them to carry out a scheme of that importance."

"There is terrible trouble about the kidnapping," said the minister. "I have brought you here to take you off the trust and put you on to that."

Larry laughed. "You can safely retain me on the trust work," he said dryly. "All the bad crimes that will be committed in this country during the next twelve months will bear the indelible hall mark of that organization."

"You know the circumstances of the kidnapping?" asked the commissioner.

Larry nodded. "The boy was out with his nurse in Regents Park. The nurse found herself in conversation with a lady who suddenly turned faint and had to be assisted to one of the garden chairs. When the nurse looked round, the child had gone, and a motor car was seen driving off in the adjoining roadway. No number of the car seems to have been taken. By the time the nurse had found a policeman the fainting lady had also disappeared."

"Lord Frethermore is distracted," said the minister. "He has seen me twice this morning. He had a letter from the gang; here it is."

He passed the epistle across the table. It was typewritten on thick notepaper, and ran:

I am holding your son to ransom and am demanding three hundred thousand francs for his release. The money must be paid in thousand-franc notes and delivered to a messenger, who will be a perfectly innocent agent in the matter. The method of the boy's restoration will be sent to you if you advertise your agreement in the Times.

The Knight of Industry.

"The trust!" said Larry confidently. "They have used that signature before. From what I have heard, the gentleman who is at the head of the business attends his 'board meetings' in complete armor, with lowered visor."

"Theatrical nonsense!" growled the minister.

"It is neither theatrical nor nonsensical," said Larry calmly. "In the first place he is protected against a chance pistol shot from a traitor or a hidden policeman, and he is so completely disguised that neither his face nor his figure is observable. I will take this letter, if I may." He folded it up and put it in his pocket. "I have an appointment with my specialist."

"How is the memory trouble?"

Larry made a grimace. "I haven't had a recurrence for over a week."

"Who is your doctor?" asked the minister. "Grayborn? A clever fellow. A man who has won the first place in his profession by sheer industry. Ten years ago a struggling practitioner, up to his eyes in debt through an extravagant wife. To-day, I suppose, he is making more money than any other man in his profession. The fees he charges me are prodigious—prodigious!"

"You are not making Larry very happy," smiled the commissioner, but Larry was incapable of further depression that morning.

He was ushered into the consulting room, and the specialist, without delay, went through the formal examination which Sir George Grayborn always gave to his patients.

"I think you're all right," said the doctor. "You have had no further sudden lapses of memory?"

"None," said Larry.

"Avoid excitement. I know it is a foolish thing to ask you, but remember that any undue excitement will produce that extraordinary lapse and blot out hours of memory from your life. Amnesia is a queer disease."

"Don't I know it," said Larry ruefully. "It is a nightmare to me every time I realize that all the things that happen to me after four may be completely forgotten until I recover my memory at eight. I live in dread of that little buzz in the ear which tells that memory is 'ringing off.'"

"Where are you going this afternoon?" asked the physician suddenly.

"Nowhere in particular," said Larry after a moment's thought.

"A little social recreation would not do you any harm," said Sir George. "I am going to a garden party at Regent Gardens; it is on behalf of the 'Home for Factory Girls.' Will you join me there?"

Larry had made no plans for that afternoon, and it was a rule of his life that when he had no plans he was prepared to be guided by any fortuitous development that day might bring forth.

"I will join you," he said.

"The ticket will cost you a guinea, and I will put it on my bill, which, by the way, will not be heavy," he said, looking over his shoulder as he unlocked a little cupboard behind his desk.

"You are a thought reader among other things, Sir George."

The physician did not reply. He handed the gilt-edged pasteboard to his patient.

"I will meet you at half past four," he said, "near the band stand."

Dressing for the function, Larry came to the conclusion that he might have done worse than accept the invitation. If one of his extraordinary memory lapses came on, he would have the advantage of his doctor's society and the observation which Sir George might make, and, what was no less important, the data he might supply as to what Larry did while in the dubious enjoyment of one of his periodical fits of oblivion. He dressed himself with care, for Larry was something of a dandy and was one of the best-dressed men in town. From his varnished boots, with their white, well-fitting spats, to the top of his glossy silk hat he might have stood as a model for the beaus of the world. He seldom went abroad unarmed, and now, as a final touch to his toilet, he dropped a revolver into his hip pocket. The result did not please him, for the bulge of the weapon showed under the well-cut morning coat.

He took out the revolver, and replaced it with a little Browning, with no great improvement. He put the Browning on the table. It was against his best instincts to go out without some kind of weapon, and he pulled open drawer after drawer, and finally selected a short and what was more to the purpose, flat hunting knife in its sheath. In a rough-and-tumble it might be more useful even than firearms.

He drove to the gardens, and found, as he approached the entrance, such a block of taxicabs and private motor cars that he descended and walked the rest of the distance on foot. He crushed through the turnstiles, and was immediately pounced upon by a bevy of beautiful brigands with tickets for side shows and badges and flags and refreshment vouchers.

He parted meekly with his money, and as soon as he could make his way free of the crowd he wandered to the part of the garden which he knew would be unfrequented.

It was a glorious summer day. The hot June sun was tempered by a cooling breeze, and in the bosky sidewalks, with their high hedges of flowering shrubs, he found a certain restfulness and comfort. He passed a small telephone box placed there, as an inscription informed him, for the convenience of visitors, and he marveled at the foresight and intelligence which had induced the organizers to place this very necessary connecting link with the outside world in so quiet and retiring a spot. It would be useful when he wanted to call his car.

He strolled on slowly, for he knew the path would soon turn him back to the crush, and then suddenly he saw a girl ahead of him. She was dressed in white, and her back was turned toward him. She was evidently selling something, for she had a little tray before her. He debated the question as to whether he would return, but curiosity got the better of him. Here evidently was a kindred soul who also wished to get free from the madding throng. He was walking past her when she spoke.

"Won't you buy a little rose?" said a sweet voice.

He turned round and looked her in the face, and something buzzed in his ears and memory stopped.

He knew his memory was returning, yet the sensation was as though he was beginning life at its very commencement and that all existence must date from this moment. He felt a strong wind in his face, and he knew his hands were grasping something rough and hard.

Then he realized he was sitting on a stone ledge. He looked down, and, strong as were his nerves, he nearly swooned. Then he looked back into the black, yawning chasm behind him. How had he got here? In the name of Heaven, how had he got here?

He was sitting on the top of a high chimney stack, a hundred and fifty feet above the level of the ground. He was dressed in his shirt and his trousers. He wore neither collar nor coat. His varnished boots were split and scratched, his white spats were black. He looked at his hand. It was covered with soot, and he gathered that his face was in no better state.

He had recovered something of his presence of mind, something of the coolness which he knew he had displayed through all this lapse of hours, even though the sudden consciousness of his position had temporarily shaken his confidence and nerve. He crawled back to the black funnel of the stack and looked down. He had evidently come up that way, for inside the stack, as far as eye could see down, were iron rungs firmly fixed in the masonry.

At the worst, he could go down that way again, he thought, but even as this method of escape occurred to him a thick cloud of smoke billowed up from the depths. He crept round to the other side of the parapet, and what he found brought comfort. Apparently the chimney had at some period been under repair, and there was a scaffolding here and a ladder which ran at an alarming angle to join a further ladder, which, so far as he could see by lying flat on his face and looking ever the edge, continued to the foot of the stack. He shuddered at the thought of making the descent by this method, but, bracing himself up, he swung his legs over the platform, felt for the rungs of the ladder, and began his descent.

He was halfway down before it occurred to him that some of the sections of the ladder might not be in place. It evidently had been up for a considerable time, and one rung he touched was so rotten that his foot crashed through it. Fifty feet from the ground, he did indeed find that a short length had either fallen or been pulled from its place, but by letting himself slowly down till his feet touched the top of the next section, he was able, by grasping the staples which still remained in the brickwork, to make the rest of the descent in safety.

It was not until he had reached the ground that he realized that all the time he had been carrying the knife in his hand. He carefully examined the blade, but it afforded him no clew. Possibly a careful search of the buildings would assist him. He was evidently in the yard of a disused factory. Rusty old railway lines, overgrown by weeds, discarded machine parts in the same condition, and a general air of desolation pervaded the yard, which was enclosed by a high brick wall. He looked up at the chimney, which was now sending out thick smoke. Somebody must be here, he thought, and he moved cautiously. If only he could remember what had happened in the last few hours!

He heard the whir of a motor car, and, crouching down behind a slag heap, he saw a car carrying three people pass along the factory roadway and disappear behind some low buildings, which he judged were somewhere near the gate. In this supposition he was right, for a little while later he heard the clang of the gate as it closed.

He waited for five minutes, but there was no further sign of life. The smoke was thinning, and was now but a white, tenuous mist that floated from the top of the chimney. He had already identified the building by a heap of discarded tins bearing the label of the "Boscombe Enamel Company," a derelict firm that had been out of business for many years.

There were a number of sheds, all deserted, some of them padlocked and some windowless. He reached what was evidently the engine house without being challenged. The smoke must come from the stokehole, and to the stokehole he made his way. The fire doors were hot, and the big furnace was still filled with a red, glowing mass. He picked up an iron rake and poked about the inside, and presently pulled out a small metal bracket of a familiar shape. In its pristine days it had been part of a telephone transmitter. He raked again, and drew up pieces of red-hot wire and the metal part of a telephone receiver, and shook his head. They meant nothing to him.

Leading from the stokehole was a steel door, which he pushed and which yielded under his touch. He found himself in a small room with walls of whitewashed brick. It had been newly swept, and there was a table and chair which were free from dust.

"Somebody has been here in the last half hour," said Larry to himself, and stepped stealthily forward to the next door. He listened, for he thought he heard voices. He gently pressed the door, and it opened. Somebody was speaking within.

"I'll bet you'll be glad to see his nibs again, won't you?"

The reply was so faint that Larry could not hear it.

"Well," said the voice, "if you are a good boy they'll let you go to-morrow. An' if you ever see me in the street don't you recognize me, d'ye hear? Because, if you do, I'll cut your throat, d'ye see what I mean?"

Larry balanced his knife in his hand, pushed the door open, and walked into the room. A man in his shirt sleeves was confronting a small and tearful boy, who sat upon what was evidently his bed.

Larry's heart gave a thump, for he recognized in the child the heir of the Frethermores. The man did not hear Larry's entrance, but something in the boy's frightened look—for Larry in his coating of soot was a terrifying sight—made the man spin round. As he did the detective closed in on him and dropped the point of his knife against the lower button of the guard's waistcoat.

"Hands up!" said Larry. "And quick!"

The man's hands went up. He shot a sidelong glance at a table, and, following his eyes, Larry saw the revolver and sprang for it.

"I think you know me," said the young man. "I am Mr. Loman, of the criminal intelligence department, and I am going to take you into custody on a charge of kidnapping."

"It's a cop," said the man. "But don't be so certain you are going to get a conviction, old friend."

"Not so much of the 'old friend,'" said Larry.

"I have seen your prisoner," said the commissioner the next morning, "and he has undergone at the hands of two experienced police officers something approaching the immoral and reprehensible third degree of the U.S.A., which we so often condemn, but which is not without its uses. Would you like me to reconstruct your remarkable story?"

"I wish you would, sir," said Larry earnestly. "I have been puzzling my brains over the matter, and I cannot for the life of me recall one single instant between half past four in the afternoon and eight o'clock that same night."

"Then stand by for a little wholesome reconstruction," said the commissioner. "I thought it would be an easy matter, because I had taken the precaution of having you shadowed by one of the best men at Scotland Yard, but he was unable to tell me a great deal, and I have the most important part of the story from the fellow you took in the works. You were seen to go into the shrubbery at twenty-five minutes to five, and you were followed at a respectful distance by the officer. You were seen to speak to a lady selling flowers, to pass your hand across your forehead, as though you were a little stunned, and then something seemed to occur to you; probably you recognized the girl, and you came striding back the way you had come and met Sergeant Jackson, whom you dispatched with orders to find Sir George Grayborn at the band stand. Evidently you were aware that the phase of forgetfulness was closing in upon you. You then turned back, and the sergeant, over his shoulder, saw you go into the telephone box. Why you went there is conjectural. I suggest that you intended to telephone for your car."

Larry nodded. He remembered that he had had that intention.

"The rest of the story is told by our prisoner as far as he witnessed it, or was able to learn the particulars from those who participated. You had no sooner entered the telephone box than two men sprang from the shrubbery and slammed the door, shutting you in. You will probably remember, if you saw it in the course of your wanderings, that it was without windows and that the interior was specially padded to make it soundproof."

"I noticed that," said Larry, "as I passed the box the first time."

"The moment the door closed on you you were helpless. The other men who were waiting in the shrubbery came out, lifted the box on their shoulders, and you were passed out of the gate, placed on a waiting motor lorry, and driven off. It was a very neat trick, and possibly, even if you had not gone in of your own accord, you would have been lured to that part of the garden and induced to enter the box.

"I suggest that finding yourself stifling, you remembered your knife and cut through the padding and the thin wood, and, having secured air vents, you awaited developments. You were taken to the old factory, my young friend, and this is where our kidnapping prisoner offers firsthand testimony.

"At a quarter past six in the afternoon the lorry came in, and the box was carried into the stokehole, which was already filled with an assortment of shavings, wood, and coal, and you and your box were thrust in. You must have realized your awful predicament and have set to work desperately to cut your way out. To escape through the steel door of the furnace was impossible, and I suggest that you squeezed your way along the little tunnel which leads to the chimney shaft, and that, minus your coat and hat and all unnecessary impedimenta, you climbed the interior of the stack and would probably have made a good descent, in fact, the same descent that you did make, even had you not recovered consciousness of the immediate past. I have had the works raided, and there is no doubt that this place has been hired and fitted up with the object of carrying out an extensive scheme of kidnapping. Frethermore's child says that he had been there and treated kindly since the day he was whisked off."

"The whole theory fits together," said Larry, "and I have no doubt that you are right."

"I am certain I am right," said the commissioner quietly. "I myself have been in the stokehole and have rescued—"

He rose and went to a cupboard, opened it, and took out a battered and shapeless object.

"Your stovepipe hat, Larry—"

Larry looked at the relic and laughed. "Also there were the marks of your toes against the soot in the interior of the stack, bits of the lock of the telephone box, and several other et ceteras."

Larry was thinking hard.

"The girl who sold roses," he said suddenly; "it was she."

"What?" demanded the commissioner.

"Something about her face. Something that reminded me of—"

The commissioner nodded.

"Yes, she was in it," he said quietly. "Our prisoner said she came back to the factory and went on her knees to the rascal in charge of the cremation and begged him to spare you."

"I think when I meet her," said Larry,—"and I know I have met her—the Crime Trust will be very nearly on its last legs."

CHAPTER III

THE CURE

The firm name of Lewis Plink & Gothmeyar is not unknown in the city of London. There are parts of Brazil and the Argentine where it is a household word, and the palatial offices of the firm in

Commissioner Street, Johannesburg, automatically testify to the consideration in which this great financial house is held.

Mr. Lewis Plink will best be remembered as the gentleman who presented Wesbury Cathedral with a service of gold plate far exceeding in value the ratable property of the city of Wesbury, and also as the owner of the steam yacht Hermada, which was faster than the fastest destroyer of the period and was furnished with a luxury beside which the furnishing of a millionaire's suite on an Atlantic liner was a Bloomsbury drawing-room.

Mr. Plink had many interests and his businesses many ramifications, which is natural, since it is not only impossible for a billionaire to keep all his eggs in one basket, but to confine his storage to baskets at all.

On the night of the thirtieth of June, a police constable of "C" division, who was making his round of Oxford Street, Covent Garden, discovered a door leading to the business premises occupied by John Wallington, Limited, printers, had been forced, and that, in the language of the police, an entrance had been effected. Summoning a comrade, he proceeded to make investigations. The door gave onto a little yard, a ladder was against a small building used as an ink store, a skylight had been forced, and through this one of the diligent officers of the law lowered himself, while his friend kept watch outside.

Thanks to the intelligent employment of rubber soles by the officers of "C" division, the policeman was able to surprise a wholly unauthorized visitor in the act of rummaging the manager's desk, and after a short struggle he was secured and conveyed to Vine Street police station.

It happened that Larry Loman, of the criminal intelligence department, was in the station when the prisoner arrived, discussing with the inspector one of the minor crimes which had been obviously committed by that extraordinary corporation which was subsequently known to the newspapers as the Crime Trust.

The conversation was suspended while the prisoner was pushed into the steel dock and the usual interrogation took place.

"Name?"

A little hesitation, then: "Brown—Thomas Brown."

"Age?"

"Thirty-three."

"Occupation?"

"Laborer."

"Where do you live?"

Again hesitation; then defiantly: "The Fritz Hotel."

"None of your nonsense," said the station sergeant. "Where do you live?"

"Rowton House, Kings Cross."

One of the divisional C. I. D. men had strolled in, and the prisoner caught his eye.

"Hello, Terence!" said the detective.

"You've made an error," replied the prisoner haughtily.

"His name is Terence Brien," explained the detective; "he is an old lag. He had five years for burglary at the Chelmsford Assizes in 1904. What have you been up to, Terence—the old game?"

"Never mind about the old game," growled the prisoner, and then, with an air of triumph: "You are not going to have it so easy this time, Mr. Busy; I shall have the best counsel that money can buy. I've got friends, I have."

Larry came forward, for now he was the most interested member of the audience.

"Would you like us to communicate with your friends?" he asked.

The man looked at him suspiciously.

"No, thank you, Mr. Loman," he grinned. "I know you, sir. You are not going to get any information out of me."

"You are working for the trust," said Larry. "Tell me why you went to Wallington's."

"Find out," said the man defiantly.

That Larry intended doing, and after the man had been removed to a cell he went back to the robbed office. The policeman had evidently disturbed the man before he had got very far with his work. Only a few packages of paper had been taken from the desk, and these were mainly invoices awaiting dispatch and correspondence of the previous day between the firm and its customers which had not yet been filed.

Pending the arrival of a representative of the firm, Larry took the liberty of examining the contents of the desk. One thing that had struck him from the first was the care with which the desk had been opened, and probably this had accounted for the length of time the man had taken, because he had obviously had the greater part of an hour. This fact was discovered by inquiries of a caretaker who lived opposite the works and who thought he had seen the flash of an electric lamp an hour before the burglary was discovered.

The drawer of the desk had not been forced, but it had been picked with great care. The documents taken from the drawer had not been scattered, but had been carefully placed on the top of the desk, and evidently the man had instructions to replace all that he had removed in as near as possible the same position and order as they had been when he found them. The very last package Larry removed from the desk was a registered envelope, the wax seal of which had been broken, probably by the official of the firm on the previous day. It contained a typewritten list of names and addresses running to many pages, and each sheet had been typed upon the letter-heading of Lewis Plink & Gothmeyar. It was four o'clock before a representative of the burgled firm arrived.

"Yes," he said, "that list came yesterday from Mr. Plink. We do all his private printing, and we are sending out cards of invitation for his daughter's marriage."

"Do you send out the cards?"

The representative nodded.

"The lists come direct to us. We print a separate card for each guest; that is to say, we alter the name with every impression. This is a practice of Mr. Plink when he is giving a particularly important party."

The object of the burglary was very clear to Larry. It was to obtain that list of names, and it had been committed by the order of the trust. Why was the list required? He knew Lewis Plink by reputation as an immensely wealthy man, and he remembered reading in a newspaper that the wedding presents had been valued at a fabulous sum, the present from the father of the bride taking some unusual shape. What it was he could not remember except that it was something bizarre and uncommon.

A search through the file of his papers revealed both the object of the burglary and the larger objective of the trust. Mr. Plink was a man of original views, and if they lacked something in taste they made up for the deficiency in tangible value. The bride, who was dowered with her weight in gold, had evidently fired the great financier's imagination, and Miss Louisa Plink was to receive as a wedding present her weight in treasury notes.

Larry opened a safe in which he kept a supply of ready money, took his letter scales, and weighed an ounce. He discovered that it took thirty-two treasury notes to turn the balance. If Miss Plink was an ordinarily healthy girl, she would weigh one hundred twenty-six pounds—that was one thousand and eight ounces—so that he dowry would amount to something like one hundred and sixty thousand pounds or eight hundred thousand dollars, which, in negotiable money, was a prize well worth securing. He looked at his watch. It was nearly seven o'clock, and he realized that he had had no sleep that night. He snatched three hours' rest; then, after a bath and a change, he made his way to the city office of Plink & Gothmeyar. Mr. Plink was a jovial little man, very bald, and very human.

Larry, who had been ushered in almost immediately, was waved to a seat and pressed to a cigar almost in one motion.

"Yes, it is perfectly true," said Mr. Plink, with his thumbs in the armholes of his waistcoat; "the money is at Cateby Court at this minute. It is being looked after with the other presents, and I do not think you need have any fear. I have two private detectives there day and night."

"Have you added to the list of your guests?" asked Larry.

Mr. Plink nodded.

"I sent along one new name this morning—Miss Cuthbert."

"A friend of yours?"

Mr. Plink hesitated.

"Well, not exactly a friend, but the friend of a friend," he said. "I am not at liberty to talk about her, but I can only tell you that the lady is of unimpeachable character, who has been known to my friend—whose name I am not for the moment permitted to give—for many years."

"That seems all right," said Larry after a pause. "And now I want you to add another to your list."

"You mean yourself?"

Larry nodded.

"With all the pleasure in life," said Mr. Plink, and pressed his bell. "The wedding is to-morrow afternoon at two o'clock, and the dinner is at seven. I shall expect you, Mr."—he looked at the card again—"Mr. Loman."

It was Larry's day for consulting his doctor, he remembered with a little grimace as he came into the street. He had grown to like Sir George Grayborn, and his gesture of repugnance was less dictated by an objection to the eminent nerve specialist than an indication of his resentment that he had to consult a doctor at all. He secretly hoped that Sir George would be out, but the great man, as it happened, was spending the afternoon at home, an unusual circumstance.

"I am glad you came in; I was getting bored," said Sir George, smiling pleasantly and rising to shake hands with his visitor. "Well, how is your amnesia?"

"I have not had an attack for over a week," said Larry cheerfully, and the elder man nodded.

"There will come a time when these curious lapses of yours will pass away forever," he said. "Yours is a very interesting case, about the third that I have met with in my professional career. I have, of course, had any number of patients who have lost their memory, but your peculiar disease is rather unusual." He was sitting at his table, fingering a pencil. "Your case is this—that at awkward hours of the day, without any warning save a faint buzzing sensation in your head, your memory fails. For three or four hours you are totally incapable of remembering anything which happened before the lapse began, though you are guided by a subconscious knowledge of previous happenings. At the end of your four hours you recover your memory, but now you cannot remember what happened during the period of lapse. That, I think, is your case."

Larry nodded.

"A very awkward and disagreeable complaint," smiled Sir George, "but we will pull you through." He reached out a hand and gripped the other's wrist, looking at his watch the while. "Pulse normal," he turned Larry's face to the window, "pupils react to light. Hold out your hand." Larry obeyed. "No tremors. Close your eyes. No swaying."

He applied one or two other tests, all of which were apparently satisfactory.

"You have no organic disease at all. Beyond this strange loss of memory, which is inconvenient without being dangerous, you are in perfect health. Now, tell me, what are you going to do for the next two or three days?"

Larry explained the engagement he had just made. The old man lifted his eyebrows.

"So you are going to sit in the shadow of Midas, too," he said.

"Are you going?" asked Larry in surprise.

"I attend Mr. Plink in a professional capacity," said the other dryly, "but a man more innocent of nerve I have never met. These functions amuse me. I shall probably see you there. I am glad I am going," he added after a moment's thought. "I am rather keen on seeing you while this fit of lost memory is on you. I nearly saw you the other day, and I have been vexed that I missed the opportunity."

Larry saw him the next afternoon on the platform of Charing Cross, which was thronged with Mr. Plink's guests. The millionaire had hired a special train to carry his friends to Chislehurst, and Larry and the doctor traveled down together.

"By the way, who are those young gentlemen?" asked the doctor just before the train drew out, indicating two silk-hatted young men who were strolling along the platform in laughing conversation, swinging their canes carelessly. "I know most of the people here, but I cannot place these."

"And I am afraid I cannot enlighten you," said Larry. He might have substituted "won't" for "can't", but in all matters affecting the service he was a most reticent man, and the two immaculate youths who were strolling aimlessly from carriage to carriage in search of a seat were men of his own department.

The train was met at Chislehurst by a fleet of motor cars, and the guests were whisked off to Mr. Plink's magnificent home. Larry and the professor traveled together in the same car.

"He is not a bad little fellow," said Sir Gorge. "I have known him for a number of years, and, in fact, I have been a sort of confidential adviser to the family. He is hopelessly rich, which is against him, and he has sufficient sense not to interfere with his really delightful chateau, which was built by the Duc de Lieven, who accompanied Napoleon III. into exile."

It was, indeed, a beautiful house, and if the interior was a little more ornate than the delicate lines of the architect had led the visitor to expect, that was pardonable.

Larry immediately sought an interview with Mr. Plink, and found him in his big study. To Larry's surprise, he discovered Sir George already on the spot ensconced in a deep armchair, smoking a reflective cigarette. He looked up with an amused smile as Larry entered.

"You know my friend, Sir George Grayborn," said Mr. Plink, indicating the other with a wave of his hand.

Larry nodded.

"I have no secrets from Sir George."

"Nor have I, unfortunately," smiled Larry.

"We have been friends for ten years," said Mr. Plink. "He attended my poor wife—help yourself to a cigar—you weren't so prosperous in those days, Sir George."

"Prosperity is a relative term," said the specialist. "I was perhaps happier then than I am now."

"Naturally, naturally," said the sympathetic Mr. Plink, "'it is rather curious, now that I come to think of it," he went on reflectively; "the first time I met you we had the very same accident, which we are trying to avoid now."

He looked up with a broad grin at the young police officer.

"Do you mean a robbery?" said Larry quickly.

Mr. Plink nodded.

"I lost the finest pearl necklace that has ever been seen in this country," he said with a certain amount of satisfaction—for it was a pleasure to Mr. Plink to be magnificent even in his losses. "It was taken from this study," he went on, "worth one hundred and fifty thousand pounds; disappeared in the twinkling of an eye. Do you remember, Sir George?"

Sir George nodded. "Now you mention the matter, I do remember."

"How did it occur?" asked Larry. "I don't remember hearing anything about it."

Mr. Plink shook his head.

"It was probably before your time, and it was a very simple matter. Somebody just opened the safe, took the pearls, relocked the safe—and there you are!"

"Is this the safe?" asked Larry curiously, and walked up to a massive steel structure in the corner of the room.

"You bet your life it isn't!" said Mr. Plink decisively. "I've had that safe changed. Do you remember, Sir George," he asked, "I changed it on your recommendation? There is not another like it in Europe."

He went to the door, rapidly twisted the combination, turned the handle, and the great steel door swung open.

Larry looked inside. There was nothing inside save a strong canvas sack, which was sewn at the top and bore a label in one corner.

"You can guess what this is," beamed Mr. Plink. "It is my present to my daughter. I am not showing it with the other wedding presents. I am taking no risks."

"Are you guarding the safe?"

"Night and day," replied Mr. Plink. "Did you see a man watching outside when you came in? Well, when we go out he will come back."

"An interesting safe," said Sir George.

He got up from his chair, walked to the big deposit, and twiddled the handle under the amused eyes of the millionaire.

"Nobody but myself knows the combination word," he smiled; "no other person in the world can open it."

They talked a little while before Larry made his adieux. He went back to the grounds, where the guests were promenading, and rejoined them. Here he was introduced to a very healthy and substantial Miss Plink, thoroughly enjoying all the attention she attracted and wholly self-possessed.

Larry did not attend the ceremony an hour later. He made a brief examination of the house and grounds. He found the detective on duty before the safe and two more in charge of the wedding presents, which had been displayed in the morning room, and saw nothing to arouse his suspicion.

It was an hilarious wedding breakfast. Everybody was in the best of spirits, only Larry, conscious that trouble of some kind was brewing, was anxious, alert, and observant.

"You are very thoughtful, Mr. Loman," chided his partner. "I believe you are nervous."

He smiled at the girl at his side a little ruefully.

"You are nearer the truth than you imagine, Lady Valentine," he said. "I am generally nervous when I cannot see everybody at the table. I wish Mr. Plink had been a little less magnificent in the way of table decorations."

He pointed to an elaborate silver center piece smothered with fruit and flowers, and Lady Valentine Curtenleigh beckoned a waiter.

"Oh, please don't!" protested Larry.

"Mr. Plink and I are old friends," she laughed. "You see, father and Mr. Plink are partners." She made a little grimace. "We dukes must live, you know, Mr. Loman—there!"

The center piece was with difficulty removed.

"Now I hope you will be less distrait," she went on. "If I had only known—— Why, what are you frowning at?"

Larry's frown was one of perplexity. Sitting opposite to him was a girl with a pale, clear skin and deep, thoughtful eyes.

"Who is that?" he whispered.

"That?" echoed his companion. "I was told her name, but I have forgotten. Oh, I have it—Miss Cuthbert! She is a friend of Sir George Grayborn's."

Where had he seen her before? That they had met he knew, but where? Suddenly the girl caught his eyes, and her face went a little whiter. She stared for a second, then turned her head away abruptly. Who was she? Where had he seen her before? He puzzled his brain to supply an answer, and hardly noticed that Mr. Plink had begun his speech.

"Now I want to ask a few friends to accompany me, my daughter, and her husband to my holy of holies," said the jovial voice of Mr. Plink, "to present a little present which is perhaps—er—er—unique in the history of wedding presents."

There was a little gust of laughter, a rattling of knife handles, a dozen fresh young voices raised in laughing protest, demands from familiar friends that the presentation should be public and that "Leah's" weight should be made known, and then the little party made the best of their way from the room.

Mr. Plink, his new son-in-law, his daughter, Sir George Grayborn, and Larry were the five who assembled in the study.

The detective was an interested spectator on the fringe of the group.

Mr. Plink twisted the combination and swung open the safe.

"Good God!" he gasped, for the safe was empty.

The detective swore that he had not left the room and that no person had entered since Mr. Plink and his guest had gone out.

"It is impossible that the safe could have been tampered with," said the troubled Mr. Plink; "it is fitted on a solid concrete foundation, and, as you see, it is possible to get round it."

Larry had made a most careful examination of the exterior. There were no signs of jimmy or blowpipe, no indication at all that the safe had been forced. He examined the interior, and found nothing that gave the slightest clew. The detective in charge was a well-known sergeant of the C.I.D., who had been in the service for twenty years, whose word could be relied upon and who was absolutely trustworthy.

"I can't understand it," said Larry.

He paced the garden, the professor at his side.

"What have you done?" asked Sir George.

"I have wired to London naturally, and the commissioner is coming down. Who is that lady?" he asked, suddenly catching sight of an isolated figure ahead.

"You mean Miss Cuthbert?" said Sir George. "She is an old friend of mine. I knew her father."

"Will you introduce me?" asked Larry.

Sir George hesitated, but only for a moment, and he walked toward the girl, spoke to her, and returned by her side.

"I have an idea I met you somewhere. By Jove! Wasn't it in the Botanical Gardens? You were selling roses."

She did not smile. Her eyes were fixed upon his.

"I remember, too," she said simply.

"Now that is very curious. I—" He suddenly put his hand to his head.

Sir George was eying him keenly.

"What is the matter?" he asked.

"I'm afraid this infernal attack, of mine is coming on," said Larry.

"Do you hear the noise in your head?"

Larry nodded.

The three stood without movement, save that once or twice Larry passed his hand wearily across his eyes.

"How are you?" asked Sir George after a while.

"I am all right, I think," said Larry cheerfully.

The physician took from his pocket a tortoise-shell penknife.

"Do you see this?"

"I see it very well," said Larry.

Sir George replaced the knife in his pocket.

"What did I show you just now?"

A look of bewilderment came into Larry's face.

"You didn't show me anything."

"Didn't I show you a penknife?"

"You didn't show me anything," said Larry in surprise.

The physician took his arm and signaled to the girl, and they walked toward a small plantation which stood in one corner of the ground.

"Sit down," said Sir George, and Larry obeyed. "I am going to tell you something which will interest you," he said slowly. "It gives me a remarkable sense of satisfaction to tell you this, because I know that everything I say will be forgotten three seconds after I have spoken. You may, in your present condition, be capable of continuous action, but you are wholly incapable of recalling words or impressions."

He waited a few minutes.

"What did I just tell you?" he asked.

"I'm blessed if I know," replied Larry. "Did you speak to me?"

The professor nodded to the girl, who was watching the detective with anxiety and fear.

"You are looking for the head of a great criminal organization," said Sir George. "It will interest you to know that I am that head." Again he paused. "Do you remember what I said?"

Larry shook his head.

"I heard you say nothing," he replied.

"Good!" smiled Sir George. "It will also interest you to learn that, although I am an excellent physician, the world refused to recognize my qualities until I had stolen sufficient money to establish myself as a great specialist; now it also recognizes me as a great organizer of crime. How do you imagine for the first three years of my struggle, laden down with debt, without friends, I managed to keep up my Harley Street house?"

"Father, be careful!" cried the girl in terror.

Sir George smiled again.

"He remembers nothing, my dear, and he will remember less," he added significantly, and his thin lips were hard.

"Father, you told me you would not—"

"My life depends upon ridding myself of this man," said Sir George. "Do you know what it means to me if I am detected?"

"Do nothing desperate," she pleaded.

"Perhaps you are right," he said softly. "We shall have our reward, dear; I have already booked our passage for Buenos Aires. I have done with the organization after this."

He turned again to Larry, who still sat cross-legged on the grass.

"You wonder how this last thing was done. I will tell you, and it will be amusing to watch you struggling after clews in three or four hours' time when you recover your power of sequent thought. The safe, as our friend Plink tells you, was supplied at my suggestion about a year after I began my criminal career. It was made by an American criminal who died in this country and whom I attended. It was placed in Plink's house by my own workmen, and for nine years I have been watching for a chance of a coup. Plink thinks that it has a solid steel and concrete foundation, but you would discover that the steel foundation, at any rate, is literally a hollow sham. If you turn the combination handle six times to the left, the floor of the safe turns, and all that is on the floor is precipitated to a little chamber immediately beneath. The bag of notes is still in the safe. One month every year I spend a vacation at this place while Plink is abroad. There will be no difficulty in recovering those notes. And now," said the professor, looking at his watch, "I must take you back."

Larry rose from the grass, dusted himself carefully, and obediently followed the professor from the wood.

At five-thirty that evening the commissioner arrived and interviewed Larry. He found that young officer, his head in his hands, in Mr. Plink's study, and with him was Sir George Grayborn.

"I am afraid our young friend has had one of those wretched lapses," said Sir George to the commissioner.

"When did this happen?" asked the latter. "After or before the robbery?"

"After," said Sir George. "In fact, I was with him when it occurred and have practically been with him ever since."

"Are you feeling better now, Larry?" asked the commissioner kindly.

"Oh, I'm feeling very fit," said Larry. "Will you excuse me?"

With a little nod, he walked out of the room.

The commissioner shook his head as he looked after him.

"Will he never be cured?"

"Oh, yes," replied the professor. "One of these days he will have the buzzing in his head and no more."

"You mean that it will not be followed by this extraordinary lapse of memory?"

"Just so," said Sir George, and then, as if a thought struck him, he walked to the door, threw it open, and called: "Loman!"

Larry was at the other end of the passage, and turned at the sound of his name.

"Tell my daughter I want her, will you?"

"Your daughter?" said Mr. Plink in surprise.

"Right!" cried the voice of Larry.

"Your daughter?" said Mr. Plink again.

"Yes," said Sir George quietly.

He paced the room, his head on his breast, his hands thrust deep into his trousers pockets, but offered no further explanation.

There was a tap at the door, and "Miss Cuthbert" came in.

"Do you want me, Sir George?" she asked.

"Just one moment, dear."

He drew her into a window recess.

"Take this," he said in a low voice. He handed her a bulky pocketbook. "You will find a car waiting at the end of the drive; I had it here in case of trouble. Tell Jackson to go straight to Dover. You will be in time to catch the Continental boat. If you don't hear from me, make your way to Switzerland; your passport is inside. Stay at the villa until I come. Whether it is for weeks or years, you must wait."

"Father!" she faltered.

"Do as I tell you. There is enough money there to last you for a year but you have authority to draw on my account in the Bank of Geneva for all the money you require." He stooped and kissed her lightly on the forehead "Go!" he ordered.

She hesitated a moment, and walked quickly from the room. She was descending the broad steps which led from the terrace to the grounds when she passed Larry. He favored her with a little nod and a queer, half-pitying smile.

"I shall want to see you in about half an hour, Miss Cuthbert," he said, "if you would be so kind as to come to the study."

She made no reply, and Larry walked thoughtfully into the house.

Sir George was expecting him, and had braced himself for the interview.

"You know why I have come, Sir George," said Larry quietly.

"I think I can guess," said the other.

"I am going to take you into custody on a charge of felony."

The commissioner stared from one to the other.

"What does it mean?"

"It means," said Sir George, "that I have made one great mistake and that your assistant is a very excellent actor. I think I am right in saying that for once the 'buzz' came, but you did not lose your memory."

"How did you know?" asked Larry quickly.

"You remembered that Miss Cuthbert was my daughter," said the head of the Criminal Trust and put out his wrists for the handcuffs.

"It was a clever move," said the commissioner. "Although it was fairly easy for a man who maintained a system of espionage to discover you had this wretched disease—from what I gather you are now cured—and to get into touch with you. By the way, have you traced the girl?"

Larry shook his head.

"I am not after the girl," he shortly. "I have jailed the rest of the gang, and that is enough for me."

Edgar Wallace – A Short Biography

Richard Horatio Edgar Wallace was born on the 1st April 1875 at 7 Ashburnham Grove, Greenwich. His mother, Mary Jane "Polly" Richards was born into an Irish Catholic family in Liverpool in 1843 and had worked in theatres, both as an actress in bit-parts and as a stagehand and usherette, until she married a Merchant Navy Captain, Joseph Richards, in 1867. He too had been born into an Irish Catholic family in Liverpool. His father had also been a Captain in the Merchant Navy, and his mother's family had a marine background. Mary was eight months pregnant with Joseph's child when he died at sea, and it was once the child had been born that she first turned to the stage, taking the stage name Polly Richards.

She joined the Marriott family theatre troupe in 1872. It was managed by Mrs. Alice Edgar, Richard Edgar, Grace Edgar, Adeline Edgar and Richard Horatio Edgar, Wallace's father. In late 1874 Mary and Richard Horatio Edgar had a brief sexual encounter at the party following a successful show, and she fell pregnant. Worried about the scandal which would ensue and fearing that she might forever lose her job at the troupe, she fabricated an obligation in Greenwich would detain her there for at least six months. She lived in a room in the boarding house on Ashburnham Grove until her son, Edgar, was born. She had already made preparations through her midwife for a couple to foster the child, and when Edgar was born the midwife presented her with Mrs Freeman. Her husband was a fishmonger at Billingsgate market and she already had ten children. She was happy to foster the child and for Polly to make frequent visits to see him in exchange for a small sum of money which Polly made from her work in the theatre troupe.

Wallace was now known as Richard Horatio Edgar Freeman, taking his father's forenames and his foster family's surname. Broadly speaking his childhood was a happy one. The Freemans looked after him lovingly and he had good friendships with his foster siblings, particularly Clara Freeman, twenty years his senior, who often looked after him as a child. After a few years Polly's finances tightened and she was no longer in a position to afford the fee she had been paying the Freemans. However, they had grown to love the young Wallace and opted to adopt him in order to keep him out of the workhouse. Polly could no longer visit him. George Freeman was keen to ensure that he had equal opportunities and did all he could to secure him an education at St. Alfege with St. Peter's, a Peckham boarding school. Despite his adoptive father's efforts, though, Wallace left the school aged twelve for truancy.

Instead he went to work and by the time he was fourteen or fifteen he had experience selling newspapers at Ludgate Circus, near Fleet Street, as a worker in a rubber factory, as a shoe shop assistant, as a milk delivery boy and as a ship's cook. He stole from the milk company which resulted in his dismissal, and in 1894 was engaged to a local girl from Deptford named Edith Anstree, though he broke this off and instead joined the Infantry. He adopted the name Edgar Wallace which he took from Lew Wallace, the author of *Ben-Hur*, and his medical record records a diminutive 33" chest and a stunted growth. his first posting was with the West Kent Regiment in South Africa in 1896, though he did not enjoy military life, arranging to be transferred to the Royal Army Medical Corps. Though this was a less strenuous job, it was also significantly less pleasant and so he again transferred to the Press Corps, which he found suited him far better.

He was in Cape Town in 1898 where he met Rudyard Kipling and was inspired to begin writing and publishing poetry and songs. His first collection of ballads, *The Mission that Failed!* and was enough of a success that in 1899 he paid his way out of the armed forces in order to turn to writing full time. His first work was as a war correspondent for Reuters who kept him in Africa to cover the Boer War, and then for the Daily Mail in 1900 and various other periodicals after that. It was while he was in South Africa that he met and married Ivy Maude Caldecott, who was 21 when they married in 1901, despite her Wesleyan missionary father's strong opposition to the union, for several reasons, one of which was that Wallace's writing was not turning quite the profit he had expected it would. *War and Other Poems* and *Writ in Barracks,* both published in 1900, had not proved as popular as his first collection. Eleanor Clare Hellier Wallace, their first child, died of meningitis in 1903 and, in rather deep debt, they returned to London. Wallace used his contacts with the Daily Mail to get work with them in London, electing to write detective novels as a means of making quick money.

Wallace met Polly, his birth mother, in 1903. He didn't remember her from his childhood as he had been too young when she became unable to visit, so it was as though they were meeting for the first time. She was sixty years old and terminally ill, living in abject poverty. She had come to Wallace seeking financial support, but he turned her away. She died in the Bradford Infirmary later that year. In 1904 he and Ivy had a son, Bryan. He was still writing and had completed his first thriller, *The Four Just Men*. Since nobody would publish it he resorted to setting up his own publishing company which he called Tallis Press and he published a serialised version of *The Four Just Men* in 1905. He received promotional assistance from the Daily Mail in which he ran a competition for entrants to guess the method of murder in the final chapter, with a prize of £1,000 for a correct guess. Although the paper's proprietor, Lord Alfred Harmsworth, refused Wallace the £1,000 prize money, Wallace persisted and went ahead with the competition, recklessly advertising on billboards and buses all over the country, hoping to expand his advertisements across the Empire. His worried colleagues at the Daily Mail managed to convince him to lower the prize money to £500, split into a first prize of £250, a second prize of £200 and a third of £50, but with the total cost of his advertisements nearing £2,000 he would need to sell £2,500 worth of copies before he could see any profit. He was confident that this could be achieved in just three months.

Though he had remarkable enthusiasm, it became clear that his managerial skills left a lot to be desired. It soon emerged that nowhere in the competition terms and conditions had he included a clause limiting the competition to one single winner; instead, any entrant with a winning answer was entitled to their corresponding prize money. Thus, if ten entrants guessed the first prize answer, the competition was obliged to pay each entrant £250. This error was only noticed after the competition had been closed and the solution had been printed in the final installment of the novel, meaning that not only was there no opportunity to write his way out of enormous financial obligation, but the entrants who had guessed correctly would by now have read the final chapter and know they had done so. £250 was an enormous amount of money to the average Edwardian family and those entitled to it were likely to make a lot of noise if they didn't receive their money. Despite this, Wallace's fist instinct was to attempt to ignore the issue entirely, even as he discovered that he initial calculations had been dramatically over-enthusiastic and it would take nearer to two years of continuous sales to break even at the initial cost of £2,500, let alone the new figure which included every correct guesser. Compounding the problem even further was the awful realisation that as sales continued throughout the initial three month period and Wallace approached the £2,500 break-even figure, new readers were still eligible to enter and guess correctly. Though it is unknown how much he eventually owed his readers, Lord Harmsworth found himself having to loan over £5,000 in order to protect the reputation of the newspaper, since 1906 had come around and there still hadn't been a list printed of all prize-winners. It was less a charitable act than one of a man anxious that the failure would reflect ill on his own paper. Wallace filed for bankruptcy shortly thereafter and as a token gesture to his creditors sold the rights to the novel to Sir George Newnes, a publisher and editor, for £75. In the midst of this chaos though, Wallace managed to write and published *Smithy*, which would become the first of a series of *Smithy* novels.

Following this fiascos Wallace was dismissed from the Daily Mail in 1907 when inaccuracies which were found in his reporting, resulting in libel cases being brought against the paper. That year he became the first reporter to be fired from the Daily Mail and was his awful reputation prevented him from finding work at any other papers. Despite all this, though, he travelled to the Congo Free State later that year and reported on the criminal treatment of the Congolese people by King Leopold II of Belgium and the Belgian rubber companies. Up to fifteen million Congolese were killed in various atrocities, and Wallace was asked to serialise stories based on his experiences for her penny magazine *Weekly Tale-Teller*. He and Ivy had another daughter, named Patricia, in 1908. Though his new work for *Weekly Tale-Teller* was bringing in some money, their financial situation was still dire and Ivy was occasionally forced to sell off her jewellery and possessions in order to pay for food. In 1911 his Congolese stories were published in a collection called *Sanders of the River*, which quickly became a bestseller. He would publish eleven more such collections featuring a total of 102 stories of adventure and tribal life set on the river Congo.

From 1908 he started to enjoy a revival of both his success and his reputation. The majority of his initial writing he sold outright in order to make money as quickly as possible and placate his creditors in the United Kingdom and South Africa, but as his success saw the reestablishment of his reputation he began to find work once again as a journalist, beginning in horse racing for the *Week-End*, the *Evening News* and then as an editor for the *Week-End Racing Supplement*. Following this success he started his own racing papers, *Bibury's* and *R. E. Walton's Weekly*, eventually buying his own racehorses and losing thousands gambling. His success was insufficient to support his newly extravagant lifestyle and his marriage began to fail in the light of his financial irresponsibility. He and Ivy had their last child together, Michael Blair Wallace, in 1916, and she filed for divorce in 1918 moving to Tunbridge Wells with her children.

Wallace began to fall for his secretary Ethel Violet King and they married in 1921, having a child, Penelope Wallace, in 1923, who would herself go on to become a successful crime writer. Wallace now began to take his career as a fiction writer more seriously, signing with Hodder and Stoughton in 1921.

He now began to organize his contracts more carefully, arranging for royalties and properly organized promotions, run by people more business-minded than himself. He was marketed as the 'King of Thrillers' and they gave him the trademark image of a trilby, a cigarette holder and a yellow Rolls Royce. He was truly prolific, capable not only of producing a 70,000 word novel in three days but of doing three novels in a row in such a manner. His publishers signed off on almost everything he wrote as soon as he turned it in, estimating that by 1928 one in four books being read at any time was written by Wallace, for alongside his famous thrillers he wrote variously in other genres, including but not limited to science fiction, non-fiction accounts of WWI which amounted to ten volumes and screen plays. Eventually he would reach the remarkable total of 170 novels, 18 stage plays and 957 short stories.

Wallace became chairman of the Press Club which to this day holds an annual Edgar Wallace Award, rewarding 'excellence in writing'. In 1923 he broadcast a report on the Epsom Derby horse race for the British Broadcasting Company, making him the first ever radio sports correspondent. His ex-wife Ivy had suffered from breast cancer between 1923-1924, and it eventually killed her in 1926 despite a successful operation to remove a tumour the year before. He wrote the essay "The Canker in our Midst" in 1926 which dealt, aggressively and controversially, with the problem of paedophilia in show business, describing how children were unwittingly left open to sexual abuse, and linking paedophilia with homosexuality. Its tone has been described as "intolerant, blustering, kick-the-blighters-down-the-stairs". He was appointed chairman of the British Lion Film Corporation on the back of the success of *The Ringer* and on the agreement that he give British Lion first choice on all his future work. This contract gave him an annual salary and a large amount of stock with the company, along with a stipend on all British Lion production of his work and 10% of their annual profits. This extraordinary contract gave him annual earnings by 1929 of almost £50,000, or almost £2 million in 2014.

He now became an active figure in politics, entering the 1931 general election as a Liberal contestant in Blackpool, rejecting the current government in favour of free trade. He lost the election by over 33,000 votes and went to America in late 1931, once again deeply in debt after buying the *Sunday News* which closed six months later. In America he quickly found work as a script doctor for RKO Pictures, enjoying early success with the 1932 adaptation of *The Hound of the Baskervilles*. This success, along with that of the play *The Green Pack*, established his reputation in America and he was able to see his own work adapted for film, beginning with *The Four Just Men*. His most successful theatrical work, *On The Spot*, which explores the life of Al Capone, has been described as "arguably, in construction, dialogue, action, plot and resolution, still one of the finest and purest of 20th-century melodramas". These successes led to his assignation on RKO's "gorilla picture" which would become famous as King Kong in 1933.

He worked on the first draft though he was beginning to experience severe headaches which brought about a diagnosis of diabetes. Despite taking medication to address his condition, it deteriorated in a matter of days. His wife booked him passage home but soon heard that he had entered a coma and died of his condition and double pneumonia on the 7th of February 1932 in North Maple Drive, Beverly Hills. In his honour the bell at St. Bride's church on Fleet Street tolled for the duration of the morning while the flags flew at half-mast. He was buried near his home in England at Chalklands, Bourne End, in Buckinghamshire. Once again, at the time of his death he was in severe debt, mostly to racing bookkeepers, though these debts were settled within two years thanks to the enormous royalties his estate continued to receive from his contracts. His writing has been translated into 29 languages, and is considered one of the most important bodies of Colonial writing.

African Novels

Sanders of the River (1911)
The People of the River (1911)
The River of Stars (1913)
Bosambo of the River (1914)
Bones (1915)
The Keepers of the King's Peace (1917)
Lieutenant Bones (1918)
Bones in London (1921)
Sandi the Kingmaker (1922)
Bones of the River (1923)
Sanders (1926)
Again Sanders (1928)

Four Just Men (Series)

The Four Just Men (1905)
The Council of Justice (1908)
The Just Men of Cordova (1917)
The Law of the Four Just Men (US title: Again the Three Just Men) (1921)
The Three Just Men (1926)
Again the Three Just Men (US title: The Law of the Three Just Men) (1929) a.k.a. Again the Three

Mr. J. G. Reeder (Series)

Room 13 (1924)
The Mind of Mr. J. G. Reeder (US title: The Murder Book of Mr. J. G. Reeder) (1925)
Terror Keep (1927)
Red Aces (1929)
The Guv'nor and Other Short Stories (US title: Mr. Reeder Returns) (1932)

Detective Sgt. (Inspector) Elk series

The Nine Bears or The Other Man or The Cheaters (1910)
revised as Silinski - Master Criminal (1930)
The Fellowship of the Frog (1925)
The Joker or The Colossus (1926)
The Twister (1928)
The India-Rubber Men (1929)
White Face (1930)

Educated Evans (Series)

Educated Evans (1924)
More Educated Evans (1926)
Good Evans (1927)

Smithy (Series)

Smithy (1905)
Smithy Abroad (1909)
Smithy and The Hun (1915)

Nobby or Smithy's Friend Nobby (1916)

The Yellow Snake or The Black Tenth (1926)
Big Foot (1927)
The Feathered Serpent or Inspector Wade or Inspector Wade and the Feathered Serpent (1927)
Flat 2 (1927)
The Forger or The Counterfeiter (1927)
Terror Keep (1927)
The Hand of Power or The Proud Sons of Ragusa (1927)
The Man Who Was Nobody (1927)
Number Six (1927)
The Squeaker or The Sign of the Leopard or The Squealer (US Title) (1927)
The Traitor's Gate (1927)
The Double (1928)
The Flying Squad (1928)
The Gunner or Gunman's Bluff (US Title) (1928)
Four Square Jane or The Fourth Square (1929)
The Golden Hades or Stamped In Gold or The Sinister Yellow Sign (1929)
The Green Ribbon (1929)
The Calendar (1930)
The Clue of the Silver Key or The Silver Key (1930)
The Lady of Ascot (1930)
The Devil Man or Sinister Street or Silver Steel
or The Life and Death of Charles Peace (1931)
The Man at the Carlton or The Mystery of Mary Grier (1931)
The Coat of Arms or The Arranways Mystery (1931)
On the Spot: Violence and Murder in Chicago (1931)
When the Gangs Came to London or Scotland Yard's Yankee Dick
or The Gangsters Come To London (1932)
The Frightened Lady or The Case of the Frightened Lady or Criminal At Large (1933)
The Green Pack (1933)
The Man Who Changed His Name (1935)
The Mouthpiece (1935)
Smoky Cell (1935)
The Table (1936)
Sanctuary Island (1936)

Other Novels

Captain Tatham of Tatham Island or Eve's Island or The Island of Galloping Gold (1909)
The Duke in the Suburbs (1909)
Private Selby (1912)
1925 - The Story of a Fatal Peace (1915)
Those Folk of Bulboro (1918)
The Book of all Power (1921)
Flying Fifty-five (1922)
The Books of Bart (1923)
Barbara on Her Own (1926)

Poetry Collections

The Mission That Failed (1898)
War and Other Poems (1900)
Writ In Barracks (1900)

Non-Fiction
Unofficial Despatches of the Anglo-Boer War (1901)
Famous Scottish Regiments (1914)
Field Marshal Sir John French (1914)
Heroes All: Gallant Deeds of the War (1914)
The Standard History of the War – Volumes 1 – 4 (1914)
Kitchener's Army and the Territorial Forces:
The Full Story of a Great Achievement (1915)
Vol. 2-4. War of the Nations (1915)
Vol. 5-7. War of the Nations (1916)
Vol. 8-9. War of the Nations (1917)
Famous Men and Battles of the British Empire (1917)
Tam of the Scouts (1918)
The Real Shell-Man: The Story of Chetwynd of Chilwell (1919)
People or Edgar Wallace by Himself (1926)
The Trial of Patrick Herbert Mahon (1928)
My Hollywood Diary (1932)

Screenplays
King Kong (1932, first draft of original screenplay, 110 pages) While the script was not used in its entirety, much of it was retained for the final screenplay.
The Hound of the Baskervilles (1932, British film)
The Squeaker (1930, British film)
Prince Gabby (1929, British film)
Mark of the Frog (1928, American film)
The Valley of Ghosts (192

Short Story Collections
The Admirable Carfew (1914)
The Adventure of Heine (1917)
Tam O' the Scouts (1918)
The Fighting Scouts (1919)
Chick (1923)
The Black Avons (1925)
The Brigand (1927)
The Mixer (1927)
This England (1927)
The Orator (1928)
The Thief in the Night (1928)
Elegant Edward (1928)
The Lone House Mystery and Other Stories (1929)
The Governor of Chi-Foo (1929)
Again the Ringer The Ringer Returns (US Title) (1929)
The Big Four or Crooks of Society (1929)

The Black or Blackmailers I Have Foiled (1929)
The Cat-Burglar (1929)
Circumstantial Evidence (1929)
Fighting Snub Reilly (1929)
For Information Received (1929)
Forty-Eight Short Stories (1929)
Planetoid 127 and The Sweizer Pump (1929)
The Ghost of Down Hill & The Queen of Sheba's Belt (1929)
The Iron Grip (1929)
The Lady of Little Hell (1929)
The Little Green Man (1929)
The Prison-Breakers (1929)
The Reporter (1929)
Killer Kay (1930)
Mrs William Jones and Bill (1930)
Forty Eight Short Stories (George Newnes Limited ca. 1930)
The Stretelli Case and Other Mystery Stories (1930)
The Terror (1930)
The Lady Called Nita (1930)
Sergeant Sir Peter or Sergeant Dunn, C.I.D. (1932)
The Scotland Yard Book of Edgar Wallace (1932)
The Steward (1932)
Nig-Nog and other humorous stories (1934)
The Last Adventure (1934)
The Woman From the East (1934) Co-written By Robert George Curtis
The Edgar Wallace Reader of Mystery and Adventure (1943)
The Undisclosed Client (1963)

Other

King Kong, with Draycott M. Dell, (1933), 28 October 1933 Cinema Weekly

Plays

An African Millionaire (1904)
The Forest of Happy Dreams (1910)
Dolly Cutting Herself (1911)
The Manager's Dream (1914)
M'Lady (1921)
Double Dan (1926)
The Mystery of room 45 (1926)
A Perfect Gentleman (1927)
The Terror (1927)
Traitors Gate (1927)
The Lad (1928)
The Man Who Changed His Name (1928)
The Squeaker (1928)
The Calendar (1929)
Persons Unknown (1929)
The Ringer (1929)

The Mouthpiece (1930)
On the Spot (1930)
Smoky Cell (1930)
The Squeaker (1930)
To Oblige A Lady (1930)
The Case of the Frightened Lady (1931)
The Old Man (1931)
The Green Pack (1932)
The Table (1932)

www.ingramcontent.com/pod-product-compliance
Lightning Source LLC
Chambersburg PA
CBHW061505170626
46811CB00004B/1611